Harry and the Little Robot

Story by Annette Smith

Illustrations by Richard Hoit

Harry is here.

Mom is here, too.

Jet
The Little Robot

4

A little robot is here.

The little robot

is in a box.

Click! Click! Click!

Look, Harry.

Look at the little robot!

Jet
The Little Robot

8

Click! Click! Click!

Look, Harry.

Here comes the little robot.

Harry is looking

at the little robot.

The little robot is looking

at Harry.

Click! Click! Click!

The little robot is happy.

Harry is happy, too.